RABBIT & BEAR

Attack of the Snack

STORY BY
JULIAN GOUGH

ILLUSTRATIONS BY
JIM FIELD

h
Hodder
Children's
Books

A Catalogue record for this book is available
from the British Library

Hardback ISBN: 978 1 444 93817 3
Paperback ISBN: 978 1 444 92172 4

Printed and bound in China

MIX
Paper from
responsible sources
FSC® C104740

The paper and board used in this book are made from wood from
responsible sources.

Hodder Children's Books
A division of Hachette Children's Group
Carmelite House
50 Victoria Embankment
London EC4Y 0DZ

An Hachette UK Company
www.hachette.co.uk

For Sandy, always

J.F.

●

To my friend Neil Farrell, whom I first met under a table when
we were schoolchildren. What a great day! (He was reciting
Monty Python sketches, brilliantly; and I was enchanted.)
And to his wonderful mother, Una Farrell, who took me in,
and fed me, and gave me a key to their Galway home (and
let me sleep there for months), at a time in my life when I was
particularly bedraggled, having been chased out of the next
valley by killer burping owls.

J.G.

One summer's day, Rabbit and Bear were
swimming in the lake.

"This," said Rabbit, "is the best day ever."

Then a Thing whizzed over their heads.

The Thing screamed, hit a tree, and fell into the water.

SPLASH!

WOOO₀₀₀OOO₀₀₀OOO!!!

"How VERY interesting," said Bear.

"Aaargh! URRGH! Horrible!" said Rabbit.

"I wonder what that was?" said Bear.

"*That* was the most hideous thing in the world," said Rabbit, "and *this* is the worst day ever."

The Thing popped back up.

Rabbit grabbed Bear's chin, and pulled.

"If I could just ..." said Rabbit, "... use your face ... as a ladder ..."

Rabbit climbed up
Bear's face, and sat on
her head. Safe!

"Thanks," said Rabbit.

Bear lifted the soggy
Thing out of the water.

"Do you know what
this is, Rabbit?"

"Of course I do," said
Rabbit. "It's a ..."

Rabbit scratched his head.

"It's a ..."

Rabbit scratched his bum.

"It's a ..."

OK, better say *something*!

"It's a Trumpwig! A Taxbill! A Wetfart!"

"It's a *what*?" said Bear.

"OK, OK, I *don't* know," said Rabbit. "I just made up the scariest words I could think of."

Bear carried the Mysterious Thing ashore.

She tipped it upside down until water fell out of it. The Thing gave a little cough. And then a little sigh. And then a little snore.

"A Thing, with feathers ..."
said Bear. "Is it a bird?"

"Maybe it's one of Woodpecker's cousins, from the next valley," said Rabbit.

Bear rolled the Thing over.

"Wow!" said Rabbit. "It hit the tree so hard, its face went *flat*!"

"Let's take her to Woodpecker," said Bear.

They followed the noise of
Woodpecker wood-pecking, till
they got to the giant sandpit.

"Yum! Yum! Yum!"

Woodpecker was in a hollow tree stump, eating delicious grubs.

"Hey Woodpecker," said Rabbit.

"Your cousin banged her face flat."

Woodpecker flew down to look.

"That's not a wood wood woodpecker!" she said. "I think it's an ow ow owl! My grandmother told me they've got flat flat flat faces!"

"An owl!!!" said Rabbit. "Owls are *dangerous*!" He jumped backwards, away from the small, soggy owl, and landed in some stinging nettles.

OWWA! MY BUM!

He jumped sideways, and landed
upside down in some spiky brambles.
"See?" said Rabbit. "See how
dangerous owls are?"

"I've never seen an owl before," said Bear.

"Ex! Ex! Exciting!" said Woodpecker.

"*Exciting?!* It's terrifying!" said Rabbit. "My grandfather told me all about owls!" Rabbit pointed at the tiny, sleeping owl. "Owls are six foot tall! With claws like swords! And they eat you ALIVE! And the next day, they BURP UP YOUR BONES!"

"One bone at a time, or all of them at once?" asked Bear, interested.

"All at once!" said Rabbit. "Burped up in a neat little parcel, wrapped in YOUR OWN SKIN, like a birthday present MADE OUT OF YOU!"

16

"No! No! No!" said
Woodpecker. "My grand
grand grandmother told me
owls are incredibly Wise
and Clean and Kind Kind
Kind and Smart Smart
Smart and smell of mint."

SNIFF

"Nonsense!" said Rabbit.

Bear sniffed the owl. "I don't smell any mint."

"The only thing this owl smells of is BEING HORRIBLE," said Rabbit.

"Um ..." said Bear, "have either of you ever *met* an actual owl?"

"Of course I, er ... haven't," said Rabbit.

"Not an Ak! Ak! Actual owl ..." said Woodpecker.

"But that is not the point!" said Rabbit and Woodpecker together. "I know *exactly* what owls are like!"

"Wise and Wonderful!" said Woodpecker.

"HURTFUL and HORRIBLE!" said Rabbit.

He shouted this so loudly, Woodpecker fell over backwards.

"Hey! Hey! Hey!" said Woodpecker. "That's rude rude rude!"

And she flew away.

"Hah!" said Rabbit.

"I won the argument!

With my brilliant ideas!"

21

"I don't think you won the argument," said Bear doubtfully. "I think you just shouted the loudest."

"SAME THING!" shouted Rabbit. Wow, shouting was fun.

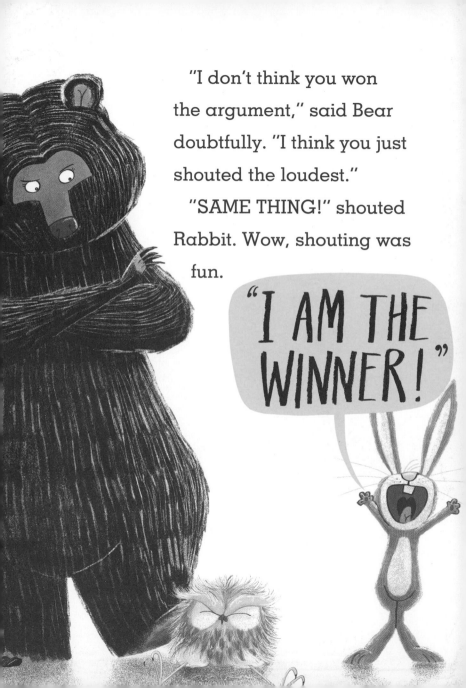

"I AM THE WINNER!"

He shouted so loudly
that other animals
started running
towards the sandpit
to see what was
happening. Except
Mole, who started
digging.

"So what did you win?" asked Mouse, and poked Owl in the tummy so hard that the sleeping Owl farted.

"Oh no! It's a Wetfart!" said Vole.

"WORSE!" said Rabbit. "It's ... an owl! A seven foot tall burping killer!"

The other animals looked
at the tiny, snoring owl and
gasped.

Then they looked again.

"It looks ... small," said Mole.

"And damp," said Mouse
in her squeaky voice.

"Did she kill *you*, Rabbit?" asked Vole, nervously. "With a giant burp?"

"Worse!" said Rabbit. "She threw me into the nettles! Look!" And Rabbit showed them his stung bum.

"Ugh!" "Awk!" "Horrible!" said the other animals, and covered their eyes.

"Oh, *bad* Owl!" said Vole.

"Er, Rabbit, that's
not really what
happened," said
Bear, but the other
animals were too
excited to listen.

27

Mole was getting grumpy in the blazing sunshine. "We must do something about this owl!" he said. "She is making me too hot!"

"Tickle her hard!" shouted Mouse.

"Tell her she is naughty! In a big angry voice!" shouted Vole.

"No!" said Rabbit.
"Even better! Throw the
terrible Owl in Prison,
before she wakes up,
and eats us, and burps
up our bones, and uses
them to decorate her
home for Hallowe'en!"

"Yes!" said Mole
and Mouse and Vole.
"Throw her in Prison!
Hurrah!"

There was a pause.

"What's a Prizzin?" said Vole.

"A Prison is a place where you can lock up EIGHT FOOT TALL KILLER BURPING OWLS," said Rabbit.

"Hurray!" cheered the animals.

All except Bear.

Bear leaned over and whispered to Rabbit, "Wouldn't it be *fairer* to wait till the owl wakes up? And then talk to her? She might be ... nice."

"You are being very reasonable. And sensible. And calm," said Rabbit to Bear.

"Oh, thank you," said Bear, relieved.

"*Stop it at once!*" said Rabbit fiercely. "I am protecting the valley, and keeping us safe! Go away if you won't help."

Bear sighed. She didn't want to fight
with Rabbit. Over Rabbit's shoulder, Bear
spotted some blueberry bushes. And mint.
"Well, I suppose I do need breakfast."

Bear wandered off.

"Now what?" said the other animals.

Rabbit hopped up on to the hollow
tree stump.

"I accuse this nine foot tall owl of stinging
bums with nettles!" shouted Rabbit.

"Boooo!" shouted Mole and Mouse and
Vole. "Bad Owl!"

"I accuse this owl," shouted Rabbit, "of …
of … of millions of crimes against rabbits
and mice and moles and voles and plants
and ants and trees and bees and land and
sand and …!"

"Boooo!"

"I accuse this owl ..." Rabbit paused dramatically, and the animals all held their breath, "... of being an OWL!!!" said Rabbit.

"BOOOO!" said all the animals. "Worst crime ever!"

The tiny owl snored, and rolled over in her
sleep.

"Throw this wicked owl in Prison!"
cried Rabbit.

Everybody started cheering, then stopped.

"We don't have a Prizzin," said Vole.

Mouse pointed at Owl, and shouted, "I accuse you of ... not building a Prison!"

"Booooooo!" shouted the animals. "Crimiest crime ever!"

"I've an idea!" said Mole.
"We can put Owl … in the
hollow tree stump!"

"Hurray!"

And all the little animals
rolled the small, wet,
sleeping Owl into the hollow
tree stump.

"Lock her up!"

Mole and Vole jammed sticks into the soft wood.

Rabbit and Mouse wrapped the tree in spiky brambles.

"Hurray!"
the animals shouted.
"The wicked Owl is
in Prison!"

Bad, bad Owl!" said Vole, and threw a blueberry at Owl.

It bounced off her tummy.

Owl opened one eye.

"The Prisoner is waking up!" said Mouse.

Owl opened the other eye.

The animals gasped and stepped back.

Owl picked up the
blueberry, and ate it.

Then she shook the water
out of her feathers, until she
looked like a bird again.

"Hmmm," said Bear,
wandering back. "That's a
funny-looking house."

"Whoooo ... Whoooo ... Whoooo used my head as a bongo drum?" said Owl, feeling the bump on her head.

"You hit your head on a tree," said Bear, still munching berries.

"Oh yes," said Owl. "I was flying tooooooo ... tooooooo ... tooooo fast ... Am I dead?" She looked around her, at the inside of the rotten tree. "If this is Heaven ... I'm *very* disappointed."

"No," said Rabbit importantly, "you are in Prison."

"Oh dear," said Bear. She shouldn't have left Rabbit in charge ...

"In PRISON?" said Owl. "Did I commit a
crime in my SLEEP?"

"Um," said Mouse.

"What did I doooooo ... dooooo ... dooooo
wrong?"

"Er ..." said Mole, and looked down and shuffled his paws.

"She doesn't LOOK like a nine foot tall burping killer," whispered Vole.

"Did I drop litter?" said Owl. "I can pick it up."

"No," said Mole, "we just thought ... you might kill us, and, you know, eat us, and um ... burp up our bones."

"Wait," said Bear. "All of you put this little owl in prison because you thought she might *eat* someone in the *future*?"

"Yes," said Vole.

"You think I'm a hungry, time-travelling criminal?!" said Owl.

"No …" Mouse felt strangely
embarrassed.

"So why am I in Prison?"

Rabbit was starting to feel he had made a
terrible mistake. He didn't like the feeling.

"How much do you know about owls?"
said Owl.

"Er …" said Mole.

"Owls are ten foot tall!"
shouted Rabbit, but now
shouting didn't make him feel
better. It made him feel worse.

A little voice, deep inside him,
said, what if you are *wrong*?

"THEY'RE KILLERS!" Rabbit
shouted, even louder, to silence
the little voice. "WHO BURP!"

"Well, OK, true, Horned Owls are big, and eat rabbits," said the little owl. "And Eagle Owls – big. Fish Owls are very big. And the Great Grey Owl is very, very big. *Their* wings can stretch five foot wide."

The animals gasped, and stepped backwards until they bumped into Bear.

Bear's tummy full of blueberries rumbled.

"But I'm not that kind of owl," said Owl.

"Don't listen to the eleven foot tall killer!" shouted Rabbit, and he shut his eyes, to check the pictures in his head. Yes, owls were big and mean and ... and ... and ... HORRIBLE! "They're all the same!"

"No, we're *not*," said Owl. "There are teeny, tiny owls tooooo, tooooo, tooooo. Elf Owls! Pygmy Owls! And *me*. I'm pretty much the smallest owl there is. And I eat *fruit* and *insects*. Come here and see, you big, mean rabbit."

Me, *big*? Me, *mean*? Rabbit opened his eyes, put up his fists, and walked very, VERY slowly up to the prison bars.

Owl raised her wing, and pushed it out between the bars and the brambles, till it just reached Rabbit's nose.

"See? Yooooou ... yooooooou ... yooooooou are bigger than me."

"Oh, your feathers
are *soft*," said Rabbit,
dropping his fists. "I
thought they would be
hard, and sharp as
knives."

Bear sighed. "Just let
Owl out of prison, Rabbit.
You made a mistake,
that's all. It's OK."

"No, it's not!" said Rabbit. His next thought was more scary than a Giant Killer Burping Owl snacking on an elephant.

"If I made a mistake ... then I'm not *perfect*. And you won't like me any more."

"*What?*" said Bear. "It's exactly the opposite, Rabbit! NOBODY is perfect, EVER. We *all* make mistakes. We *have to*! It's how we learn!"

"YOU don't make mistakes, Bear," said Rabbit.

"Yes I do! I just made one! I should have stopped you being so silly with Owl earlier, but I didn't want to argue with my friend." Bear's tummy rumbled again. "AND I just made the mistake of eating too many blueberries ... Look, just let Owl go."

"But ..." said Rabbit. "What if she's a Horrible Giant Killer Burping Owl! They ARE real!"

"They may be real IN SOME
OTHER VALLEY," said Bear.
"But here and now, they are just
an idea in your head. Look at
the *real* owl in *front* of you."

Rabbit looked.

She was small. And friendly.

Nothing like the idea in his head.

Oh *dear*, thought Rabbit. Why did I
put this lovely little owl in Prison?
Maybe Bear was right.

"I ..." said Rabbit, "made a ..."

Whew, it was very hard to say it. It felt like coughing up a rock.

"... mistake."

Oh, wow. It WAS like coughing up a rock! A huge weight had left Rabbit!

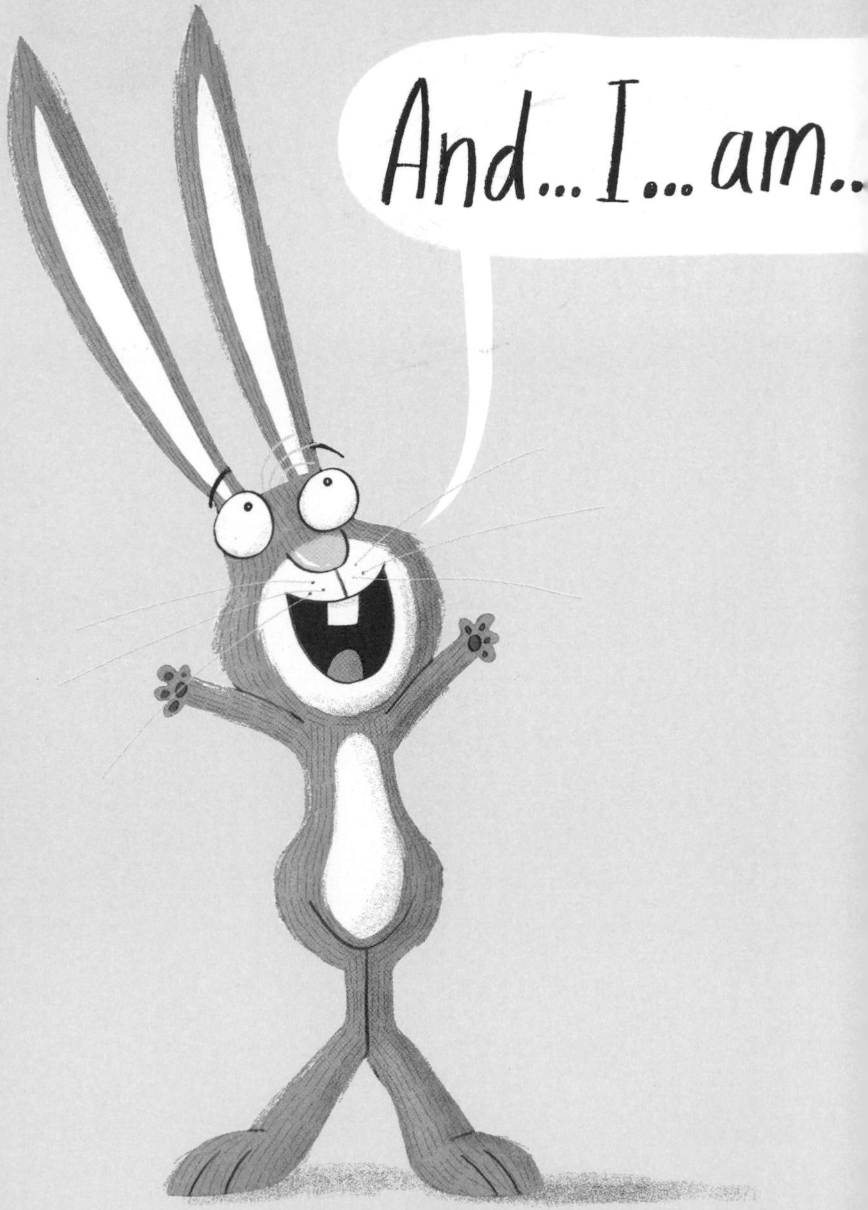
And... I... am..

SORRY?

An even bigger weight lifted off Rabbit! He felt lighter than air! He had to check his feet were still on the ground.

"I'm really sorry!" said Rabbit, bouncing up and down with lightness and gladness. "I'm not just saying it! I actually mean it!"

He unwrapped the brambles.

Owl stepped out, and shook her feathers.

"I'm sorry I threw a blueberry at you," said Vole.

"That's OK," said Owl. "It was delicious."

"I'm sorry I poked your tummy," said Mouse.

"That's OK," said Owl. "I like tickles."

Rabbit remembered something else.
"WOODPECKER! I'M SORRY I
SHOUTED AT YOU!" shouted
Rabbit.

Woodpecker flew back.

"That's OK," said
Woodpecker. "I Flew!
Flew! Flew! Into your
burrow, and pooed all over
your favourite chair, and
now I feel MUCH better."

"Gah!" said Rabbit.

Bear sighed. "Woodpecker …"

"OK, OK, OK, I'm sorry sorry sorry!" said Woodpecker.

Everyone said sorry to everyone else, until they were friends again.

SORRY!

SORRY SORRY SORRY

"Owl," said Rabbit.

"Can we *help* you?"

"Well ..." said Owl, "I don't have anywhere tooooo tooooo tooooo live ... Could you help me build a new home?"

"Oh ... I'd love to," said Rabbit. "But ... I can't climb trees." He sighed.

Owl laughed. "You don't know ANYTHING about owls like me! Watch ..."

And she started digging
into the soft, sandy ground.
In a few seconds she had
disappeared.

"Wow!" said Rabbit.

Owl popped back up.
"I'm a burrowing owl!"

"Oh, I can help you with
that!" said Rabbit.

"I'll help too!" said Mole.

They started burrowing.

"This sand is much nicer for digging than my old rocky island," said Owl, as they dug together.

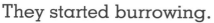

"And there are no Big, Mean, Killer Burping Owls to chase me, and try to eat me ... "

"Big owls eat *little* owls?" said Mole.

"Yes! We're their *snacks*! That's why I was flying so fast!"

"They chased you all
the way here?" said Vole.
"From the next valley?"
"Yes. Because I made a joke about
them." Owl sighed. "And Killer Burping
Owls just don't have a sense of humour."

"I have a sense of humour!" shouted Vole, excited.

Vole had only discovered she had a sense of humour the day before, when Bear had farted a tune by mistake, and Vole had laughed for three hours. Vole was very keen to use her sense of humour again.

"Can you *fart* any jokes?" said Vole.

"I could try," said Owl. "But I'm better at burps."

"Burps are good too," said Vole, generously.

"Wouldn't it be nice," said Mouse, "if we had a place just to make each other laugh ..."

"We can turn the prison into a Summer Stage!" said Vole. "For jokes!"

"A lovely idea," said Bear. "It's too hot for dancing."

Mouse and Vole pulled down all the sticks and brambles. They built a ladder from the sticks, and made the stump into a stage.

Bear made daisy chains, and hung them around the edge.

"Thunder!" said Rabbit,
looking up.

GRRRuuuMMBLE!

"No, it's my tummy,"
said Bear. "Er, I need to
do … something. In the
woods. Excuse me."
Bear trotted off.

At last Rabbit
said, "Whew,
your new home is
finished."
"Almost." Owl
looked around.

"I just need *one more thing*," she said.

At that moment, Bear came back.

Owl sniffed, in the direction Bear had come from. "What a great smell! It's exactly what I need to make my new home perfect ..."

And Owl ran into the woods.

"Oh dear," said Bear.

Owl came back rolling an enormous ball of Bear's poo.

"This is perfect!" Owl said. "Blueberry poo!"

"What," said Rabbit, "… will you do …
with that blueberry poo?"

"Cover the walls of my burrow with it, of
course," said Owl politely.

"You use *poo* as *wallpaper*!?" said Rabbit
and Bear and Woodpecker and Mole and
Mouse and Vole.

"Oh yes. It's what burrowing owls
doooooo … doooooo … doooooo. We
love pooooooo … pooooooo … pooooooo
… Don't yoooooooou … yoooooooou …
yoooooooou?"

"Let's not talk about that," said Rabbit, who had some very unusual poo habits of his own. "WHY POO WALLPAPER?"

"To attract delicious, crunchy dung beetles, of course," said Owl. "They *love* the smell of poo ..."

"You eat DUNG BEETLES?" said Mole, as he chewed on a delicious, wriggly worm. "UGH!"

Woodpecker stopped licking delicious wriggly grubs with her spiky tongue. "DUNG BEETLES?" she said. "IKKKKY! BLEKKKKY! YUKKKKY!"

"Well ... there are worse things you could eat," said Rabbit, who ate worse things every morning.

A shiny dung beetle ran towards the enormous ball of poo.

"See?" Owl picked it up and ate it. "Delicious! Crunchy! Snacks!"

"Your food *delivers itself*?" said Rabbit.

"From miles around!" said Owl. "Fast foooooo ... fooooooo ... foooooood!"

Another dung beetle ran by.

"VERY fast!" Owl ate it. "They're delicious with mint." She plucked a few leaves and ate them.

"Oh, I love you, Owl," said Rabbit, and stuck his head down Owl's tunnel to admire the wallpaper.

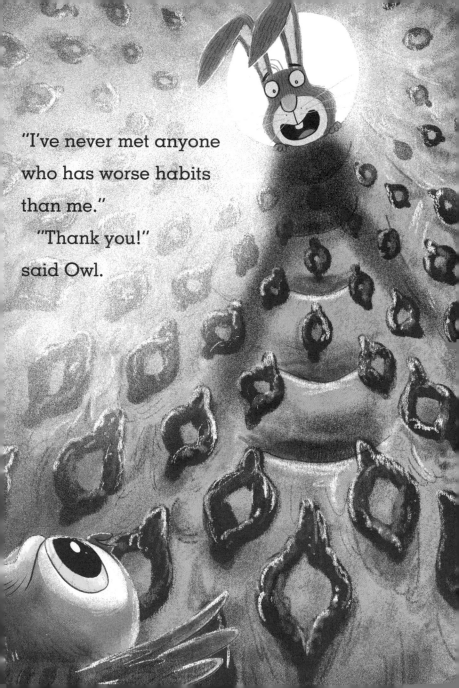

"I've never met anyone who has worse habits than me."

"Thank you!" said Owl.

"We all look normal on the
outside, Rabbit," said Bear. "But,
just like our burrows, and caves,
and tunnels, and nests …"

"We're weird on the inside!"
said Rabbit.

"Yes," said Bear. She smiled.
"And that's OK."

Soon the Summer Stage
was finished. The animals got
comfortable as they waited for
Owl's show to begin.

"Hullooooo ... Rabbit ..."
said Tortoise, arriving behind
Rabbit. "I came ... to seeeee ...
what alllll ... the shouting ...
was aboooout ..."

"SHOUTING?" said Rabbit.
"That was hours ago!"

"Yes ... I knooooow ..." said
Tortoise. "I ... rrrran ..."

Tortoise smiled, very slowly and proudly.

"I think ... I set ... a newwww ... rrrrrecord."

"Well, you are just in time!" said Rabbit.

"I need a chair."

Owl stepped on to the stage.

Everyone cheered.

"Tell a joke!" said Vole.

"What's brown and sticky?" said Owl. All the animals gasped.

"A STICK!"

All the animals, except Vole, laughed.

"I don't understand that joke," sighed Vole. "It's much too complicated."

"It's OK," said Owl. "I have *other* jokes."

And then Owl
burped a tune. It was the loudest,
longest, most musical burp anyone had
ever heard, and it smelled of mint.

Vole fell over laughing, and Rabbit
fell off Tortoise.

RRRRP!

"See, I was right!" said Woodpecker, helping Rabbit back up. "Mint! Mint! Mint!"

"We love you, Owl!" shouted the crowd.

Owl took a bow. "Thank yooooooou ... yooooooou ... yooooooou!" she said. "I love you tooooo ... tooooo ... tooooo ..."

And then she told a
joke about Giant Killer
Burping Owls that was
so funny Rabbit got
hiccups, Mole fainted,
and Mouse sneezed in
Vole's ear.

HiC!

"I was wrong about Owl this morning," said Rabbit, when he'd stopped hiccupping. "But I was right about ONE thing."

"What's that?" said Bear.

Rabbit waved his hands at all the animals laughing under the summer sky.

"This really IS the best day ever!"

Julian Gough

© Andreas Riemenschneider 2015

Julian Gough is an award-winning novelist, playwright, poet, musician and scriptwriter.
He was born in London, grew up in Ireland and now lives in Berlin.

Among many other things, Julian wrote the ending to **Minecraft**, the world's most successful computer game for children of all ages.

He likes to drink coffee and steal pigs.

Jim Field is an award-winning illustrator, character designer and animation director.
He grew up in Farnborough, worked in London and now lives in Paris.

His first picture book, **Cats Ahoy!**, written by Peter Bently, won the Booktrust Roald Dahl Funny Prize. He is perhaps best known for drawing frogs on logs in the bestselling **Oi Frog**.

He likes playing the guitar and drinking coffee.

Jim Field

© Sandy Foucherand 2016

LOOK OUT FOR MORE

RABBIT & BEAR

BOOKS COMING SOON!

FIND OUT WHAT HAPPENS NEXT IN:

A Bite in the Night

'*Rabbit's Bad Habits* is a breath of fresh air in children's fiction, a laugh-out-loud story of rabbit and wolf and bear, of avalanches and snowmen. The sort of story that makes you want to send your children to bed early, so you can read it to them.'
Neil Gaiman

'A perfect animal double-act enchants.'
Alex O'Connell, *The Times* book of the week

'Sure to become a firm favourite.'
The Bookbag

'What a treat this little book is! Not only does it have a funny and warm story that is full of heart, it is also gorgeously presented... Lots of fun, highly recommended.'
Reading Zone